Samuel French Acting Edition

An O. Henry Christmas

A Christmas Musical

Adaptation, Music, and Lyrics by
Peter Ekstrom

I0591819

SAMUEL FRENCH

SAMUELFRENCH.COM   SAMUELFRENCH.CO.UK

FOR PRODUCTION ENQUIRIES

UNITED STATES AND CANADA
Info@SamuelFrench.com
1-866-598-8449

UNITED KINGDOM AND EUROPE
Plays@SamuelFrench.co.uk
020-7255-4302

Each title is subject to availability from Samuel French, depending upon country of performance. Please be aware that AN O. HENRY CHRISTMAS may not be licensed by Samuel French in your territory. Professional and amateur producers should contact the nearest Samuel French office or licensing partner to verify availability.

Please refer to page 72 for further copyright information.

First Produced by
The Barter Theatre, Abingdon, VA
Richard Rose, *Artistic Director*

O. Henry's

The Last
Leaf

Adaptation, Music & Lyrics
by

PETER EKSTROM

The Doctor . . . . MARK DELABARRE

Sue . . . . STEPHANIE POPE

Johnsy . . . . GLORY CRAMPTON

Behrman . . . . PETER JOHL

Pianist: *Bob Goldstone*

Directed by John Hardy

This work is dedicated to Mark Davis.

CAST OF CHARACTERS

THE DOCTOR:
  non-singing (doubles as JIM in GIFT OF THE MAGI)

  The DOCTOR is a young man in his mid-thirties. He provides narration for the piece, talking directly to the audience as well as stepping into the action. He never leaves the stage, but watches when he is not involved.

SUE:
  Mezzo-Soprano

  SUE is in her mid to late twenties. She is a sculptor but does commercial art (ad sketches) to make ends meet. She is nurturing and warm, completely devoted to her friend. The older sister type.

JOHNSY:
  Soprano (doubles as DELLA in MAGI)

  JOHNSY is in her early or mid-twenties. She is an oil painter whose dream is to travel someday to Italy and paint the Bay of Naples. She is philosophical but sometimes light-hearted and gay. She is smaller than SUE, with fragile features.

BEHRMAN:
  Character Baritone

  BEHRMAN is "past sixty", a failure in art. German. He is always ready to paint his "masterpiece" but so far: an empty canvas. He earns money by posing for artists (like SUE) who can't afford a professional model. Perhaps he has a long beard. An Imp-satyr, he is always drunk on gin.

TIME: 1905, April and November

PLACE: A third floor garret, Greenwich Village, NYC

SET:

The main feature of the set is a very large window that spans both garrets and looks out onto the brick wall upon which THE VINE is growing. The window is a source of sunlight and moonlight and has a curtain the full length of it, in SUE and JOHNSY's part at least, which can be drawn open and shut.

The set is in three sections, the largest, and most of the stage being SUE and JOHNSY's garret. There is a door from the stairs to it. It has slopes and angles. The furnishings are simple (but 1905) as these are young artists just barely making it. SUE and JOHNSY transform their garret during their first song. There is an iron bed where JOHNSY sleeps that views THE VINE through the window. The other bed is perhaps built into an alcove or window. A small kitchen and eating area, space for a small easel for JOHNSY and a small work area for SUE. The whole place is not very big. There is a chair by the bed, perhaps a few more pieces of furniture. And there is the life-size head/bust of SUE's mother.

The other section of any size represents BEHRMAN's studio next-door. A few chairs, a table, and an easel on which is a huge canvas draped from view.

The third section is a place downstage where the DOCTOR talks from while he narrates. He might have a mission chair to sit in while he is observing the action. Or there is no section for him and he just wanders.

SIMPLE and ROMANTIC are key words. Also, INVENTIVE, since they are all artists. This can be realistic 1905 or impressionistic 1905. But it must be 1905!

If the impressionistic approach is used, there could be a cyclorama upstage on which the vine hangs, and SUE and JOHNSY could play it downstage as if looking out the window.

SCENE/SONG BREAKDOWN

The Last Leaf

Scene 1

(There is a Mini-Overture. Music Cue #1. The music continues as the DOCTOR speaks to audience. Music Cue #2.)

DOCTOR: Good evening. My name is William Fletcher, and I'm a Doctor of Medicine. Our story begins, and ends, in the City of New York: In a little district west of Washington Square the streets have run crazy and broken themselves into small strips called "places." These "places" make strange angles and curves. One street crosses itself a time or two. An artist once discovered a valuable possibility in this street: Suppose a collector with a bill for paints, paper and canvas should, in traversing this route, suddenly meet himself coming back, without a cent having been paid on account! So, to quaint old Greenwich Village the art people soon came prowling, hunting for north windows and eighteenth-century gables and Dutch attics and low rents. Then they imported some pewter mugs and a chafing dish or two from Sixth Avenue, and became a "colony." *(The music continues as lights come up on SUE and JOHNSY's studio.)* At the top of a squatty, three-story brick Sue and Johnsy had their studio.

(The underscoring stops.)

SUE: *(Off stage)* Just one more flight! Come on, you can make it, Johnsy!

DOCTOR: "Johnsy" was familiar for Joanna. They had met at the *table d'hote* of an Eighth Street "Delmonico's" and the joint studio resulted.

(The DOCTOR continues to watch the play as lights come up more on the garret. We see SUE coming up steps, then coming through the door lugging a heavy trunk.)

SUE: *(To JOHNSY, off stage.)* Want me to help?

JOHNSY: No! No! That's alright. I can manage .....
AAAAAAAAAHH!!! *(There is a loud shriek from JOHNSY off stage followed by the sound of falling luggage, then the sound of JOHNSY laughing and muttering, ad lib. SUE runs out and they both enter carrying the luggage and boxes, laughing. JOHNSY looking about.)* Oh Sue! It's wonderful!

SUE: I thought you'd like it. I've only been here a day. See? *(She points to some boxes.)* I'm still not unpacked.

JOHNSY: So much light!

SUE: Yes, but I'm afraid not much of a view. Just that old brick wall and one lonely vine. English Ivy, I think ...

(JOHNSY looks out window.)

JOHNSY: It's always nice to have a little bit of green.

SUE: *(Clearing a space.)* Here ... You take the bed and that side. I've started to set up over here by the stove.

JOHNSY: But it's darker over there.

SUE: I don't need as much light for my sculptures as you do for your oils.

JOHNSY: Thank you, Sue. You're so nice to me.

SUE: Why shouldn't I be?

(MUSIC CUE #3. During this song they unpack their things, taking out hangings, photos, personal items, and pieces of their art work so that the set is decorated and transformed by the end of the song into a colorful, eclectic – but meager and inventive – artist's studio.)

SUE:
(Sings as an aside, directly to the audience as well as to herself.)
WHAT'S SHE LIKE?
IS SHE ALWAYS FRIENDLY?
IS SHE NICE?
IS SHE WARM LIKE A STREAM OF SUNLIGHT?
OR IS MY ROOMMATE MADE OF ICE?

CAN SHE BE THE FRIEND I'VE WAITED FOR?

SOMEONE WHO CAN CHEER ME UP IF I FEEL BLUE?
(She steps back from something she has just hung and sings to
JOHNSY:)
I THINK THAT LOOKS PRETTY
DON'T YOU?
    JOHNSY:
(Sings to audience and herself.)
WHAT'S SHE LIKE?
IS SHE ALWAYS GENTLE?
IS SHE TRUE?
CAN I TRUST ALL THIS FOND AFFECTION?
WILL WE BE FRIENDS OUR WHOLE LIVES THROUGH?

CAN I TELL HER MY MOST SECRET THOUGHTS?
SHOULD I OPEN UP?
WE'LL HAVE TO WAIT AND SEE
(She sings to SUE, in answer to her question.)
THAT LOOKS VERY PRETTY
TO ME ...

(The music continues under this:)

    DOCTOR: The hours and days flew by, and before they knew
it, a week had gone! Sue and Johnsy were having a grand time,
settling in, making a little home for themselves.
    SUE:
(To JOHNSY)
TELL ME, JO
WHERE DID YOU GET THIS PAINTING?
    JOHNSY:
IT'S MY CREATION
    SUE:
VERY NICE!
LET'S HANG IT BY THE WINDOW
    JOHNSY:
OH, NO! LET'S HIDE IT!
    SUE:
WHAT A SKY!

HOW DID YOU GET THAT COLOR?
>JOHNSY:

IT'S REALLY NOTHING
>SUE:

I PREDICT:
SOMEDAY YOU WILL BE FAMOUS
(Spoken) I'm impressed!
>JOHNSY:

(To herself and audience.)
SOMETHING'S WRONG
I DON'T THINK SHE LIKES ME
AM I RIGHT?
I AM FILLED
WITH TOO MANY WORRIES
BETTER SMILE BACK AND BE POLITE
>SUE:

(To herself and audience.)
LOOK AT HER:
SHE HAS THE SADDEST SMILE.
WONDER IF SHE'S REALLY HAPPY DEEP INSIDE?
WHAT IS IT SHE'S TRYING TO HIDE?

(Music continues.)

DOCTOR: More weeks passed – and Sue and Johnsy were quite happy with the living arrangement. In fact, something very special was beginning to develop.
>JOHNSY:

(At a life-size clay bust.)
TELL ME, SUE
WHERE DID YOU GET THIS SCULPTURE?
>SUE:

IT'S MY CREATION
>JOHNSY:

WHAT A FACE!
WHO DID YOU GET TO MODEL?
>SUE:

MY DARLING MOTHER

JOHNSY:
YOU'RE SO GOOD!
YOU COULD MAKE LOTS OF MONEY
    SUE:
LET'S CROSS OUR FINGERS
    JOHNSY:
I PREDICT:
SOMEDAY YOU WILL BE FAMOUS
    SUE: *(Spoken)* One can hope!

    SUE: *(To audience and self.)*   JOHNSY:
WHAT'S SHE LIKE?   OH,
IS SHE ALWAYS FRIENDLY?   I TRY TO BE NICE
IS SHE NICE?   WHEN I FIRST MEET
IS SHE WARM   A STRANGER
LIKE A STREAM OF SUNLIGHT
OR IS MY ROOMMATE   I TRY TO BE
    MADE OF ICE?   FRIENDLY

    BOTH:
CAN SHE BE THE FRIEND I'VE WAITED FOR?
SOMEONE WHO CAN CHEER ME UP IF I FEEL BLUE?
    SUE :
(To JOHNSY)
NEVER HAD A ROOMMATE LIKE YOU

(The music continues.)

    JOHNSY: What do you mean by that?

    SUE: I don't know. I guess, it's just I've only known you for a short time, and yet I feel I've known you forever.

    JOHNSY: Me, too. It's funny, isn't it? ... how that sometimes happens.

    SUE: I like the feeling.

    JOHNSY: The world is rough. It's good to have a friend.

    SUE: It's good to feel like this.

    JOHNSY: *(Sings to SUE)*
HOW I LONG FOR SOMEONE TO CONFIDE IN

SUE:
(Sings to JOHNSY.)
YOU'VE GOT ME
    JOHNSY:
SOMEONE WHO CAN HOLD ME IF I'M FRIGHTENED
    SUE:
TAKE A CHANCE
    JOHNSY:
IT'S NOT EASY FINDING FRIENDS WHO LOVE YOU
    SUE:
DON'T I KNOW!
    JOHNSY:
IF WE'RE LUCKY WE'LL BE FRIENDS FOREVER
    SUE:
THEN WE WILL!

SUE: *(To self and audience.)*
MY ROOMMATE MUST BE
A VERY SPECIAL PERSON

MY HEART IS FILLED
WITH FOND AFFECTION

JOHNSY:
WHAT'S SHE LIKE?
IS SHE ALWAYS
    GENTLE?
IS SHE TRUE?
CAN I TRUST
ALL THIS FOND
    AFFECTION?
WILL WE BE FRIENDS
    OUR WHOLE
    LIVES THROUGH?

    BOTH:
CAN I TELL HER MY MOST SECRET THOUGHTS?
SHOULD I OPEN UP?
WE'LL HAVE TO WAIT AND SEE
    SUE:
WON'T YOU BE A SISTER TO ME?
    JOHNSY:
COME, COME THIS WAY
COME TO ME ...

(They do some little friendship ritual with their pinkies or finger

tips, and end in an embrace on the last beats of the song.
BEHRMAN is heard in the hall singing "Ode To Joy" in
drunken glee. Music Cue #4. This serves as underscore until
he knocks on door.)

SUE: Listen! There's that man again from across the hall. I
wonder if he'll come in this time if we invite him?

JOHNSY: Why do you suppose he keeps to himself so much?

SUE: I've never been able to figure out the Germans.

DOCTOR: Old Mr. Behrman was the German painter who
occupied the garrett across the hall. He would lock himself away
for days, sometimes weeks at a time, working on some
"masterpiece" or another. He always smelled strongly of juniper
berries.

(BEHRMAN stops singing and knocks on door. SUE opens door
and BEHRMAN stands there.)

BEHRMAN: Guten tag. Guten tag. Guten tag. Please allow me
to represent myself: I am Herr Behrman your cross-the-hall
neighbor.

SUE & JOHNSY: How do you do.

BEHRMAN: And you are Zue, and you must be leetle Yohnsy.

JOHNSY: How did you know our names?

BEHRMAN: I may be locked up over her with my vork, but I zee
many things in der hallway through my peep-hole! Do you invite
me in?

SUE: Why, yes ... Come in, Herr Behrman.

(BEHRMAN produces a small bouquet of posies.)

BEHRMAN: For your new studio!

JOHNSY: Oh, thank you!

SUE: They're so pretty! Would you like to sit, Mr. Behrman?

BEHRMAN: I prefer ... to valk. *(He walks around, inspecting*
their art work.) Ach! Vat a sky! How did you get dat color?

JOHNSY: Oh, it's really nothing.

BEHRMAN: Nein, nein – deez is something special ... Dis is yours? ... You are a great artist, mein schatz.

SUE: How come we've been here for weeks and you decide to come and see us today?

BEHRMAN: I have been very very busy – locked up, vorking on my masterpiece!

JOHNSY: Oh? You're a painter?

BEHRMAN: Ja, mein leibchen.

JOHNSY: What do you paint?

BEHRMAN: I paint everything – and nothing! I am an Artist! I live for Art! I vill die for Art if I have to! *(To SUE)* And you? You are an Artist, too, ja? *(He notices bust of SUE's mother.)* Ach! Look at dat! Did you do dat?

SUE: Yes, Mr. Behrman.

BEHRMAN: Ach, such beauty! It looks like my ex-wife.

SUE: It's my mother.

BEHRMAN: So you're my long lost daughter!

(He goes to embrace.)

SUE: *(Laughing)* No, I think not!

(They all laugh.)

BEHRMAN: Ah, to breathe the air! To be here on Bleeker Street surrounded by such beauty! And to be among Artists! We are all alike, you know: we have to create Art in order to live! Others can't show der emotions as easily as we. So we do it for dem in our Art! Art is life! Life is Art! I am me! You are you! Here's the gin – let's drink!

(He pulls out flask.)

JOHNSY: Oh, Mr. Behrman! We don't drink!

SUE: How about a cup of coffee? I'll get it.

BEHRMAN: Well, I suppose we could drink a toast with coffee. But it's not as effective as with gin! *(He puts flask in pocket.)* Oh, I almost forgot! *(He pulls a tube of paint from his pocket.)* For you, my leetle Yohnsy ... from my own collection.

JOHNSY: Mediterranean Blue! Oh, Sue! Oh, Mr. Behrman, I haven't been able to afford this particular blue for some time.

BEHRMAN: You must promise me never to stop painting. You are a real Artist, my new young lady friend, Yohnsy. Will you promise me never to stop painting?

JOHNSY: I promise ... Thank you, Mr. Behrman.

(JOHNSY kisses him on the cheek.)

BEHRMAN: And for you, Zudie – *(He searches pockets but comes up empty.)* Umm, ummm ... You may kiss me, too!

(Offers cheek to SUE.)

SUE: How about a nice cup of hot coffee?

BEHRMAN: Yes, yes! A cup! Let's drink a toast! *(During this scene and song, SUE fills the cups with coffee and BEHRMAN, on the sly, keeps spiking ALL the cups with gin from his flask. This happens many times during the song until by the end, they are all a bit tipsy.)* Let's drink a toast to ... to ... blue! To Mediterranean Blue!

JOHNSY: Yes! To Mediterranean Blue!

BEHRMAN: Prosit!

(They click cups and drink.)

SUE: Now let's drink to another cup of coffee!

(She refills the cups, and he gets gin into them.)

BEHRMAN: Ja, ja! To another cup of coffee!

JOHNSY: To another cup of coffee!

SUE: To another cup of coffee!

BEHRMAN: Prosit! *(They click and drink. Music starts. MUSIC CUE #5. Sings, with German accent.)*

LET'S DRINK A TOAST TO SUDIE AND TO JOHNSY
NO NICER NEIGHBORS DID I EVER MEET

IT'S TIME WE CELEBRATED YOUR ARRIVAL
TO THIS GREAT STUDIO ON BLEEKER STREET
LET'S DRINK TO ALL THE ARTISTS ALL AROUND US
OUR COLONY WILL NEVER FALL APART!
SO RAISE THE CUP!
LET'S DRINK TO LIFE, TO BEAUTY!
BUT MOST OF ALL LET'S DRINK A TOAST TO ART!
 ALL: *(Sing)*
TO ART, LET'S DRINK TO ART!
TO ART, LET'S DRINK TO ART!
LET'S DRINK A TOAST TO ART!
SO RAISE THE CUP AND BOTTOM'S UP!
LET'S DRINK A TOAST TO ART!
PROSIT!
LET'S DRINK A TOAST TO ART, TO ART
LET'S DRINK A TOAST TO ART!

(There is more drinking, spiking with gin, etc.)

 JOHNSY:
I'M SURE YOU'RE GOING TO BE A LOVELY NEIGHBOR
IT'S GOOD TO MEET YOU, FINALLY, FACE TO FACE
 SUE:
AND MAYBE SOMEDAY IF YOU WILL ALLOW IT
WE'LL GET TO SEE THE PAINTINGS IN YOUR PLACE.
 BEHRMAN:
LET'S DRINK TO ALL THE COLORS OF THE RAINBOW
LET'S DRINK TO ALL THE PASSION IN THE HEART
SO RAISE THE CUP!
LET'S DRINK TO LIFE, TO BEAUTY!
BUT MOST OF ALL LET'S DRINK A TOAST TO ART!
 ALL:
TO ART, LET'S DRINK TO ART!
TO ART, LET'S DRINK TO ART!
LET'S DRINK A TOAST TO ART!
SO RAISE THE CUP AND BOTTOM'S UP!
LET'S DRINK A TOAST TO ART!
PROSIT!

LET'S DRINK A TOAST TO ART, TO ART
LET'S DRINK A TOAST TO ART!
LET'S DRINK TO ART!
TO ART LET'S DRINK!
LET'S DRINK,
LET'S DRINK A TOAST TO ART!
TO ART, TO ART, TO ART!
LET'S DRINK,
LET'S DRINK A TOAST TO ART!
LET'S DRINK TO ART!
LET'S DRINK TO ART!
TO ART, TO ART, TO ART, TO ART!

BEHRMAN: And now – I thank you for der warm American hospitality – but I must remove myself.

JOHNSY: Thanks for coming, Mr. Behrman.

BEHRMAN: I must lock myself in an vork on my masterpiece.

SUE: Yes, thank you, Mr. Behrman. And don't wait so long to come visit us next time.

BEHRMAN: I von't, mein liebchens. I come out lots more now dat I have my two sweet young lady friends across der hall! Auf wiedersehen! Auf wiedersehen!

(BEHRMAN exits, SUE and JOHNSY begins to pick up.)

JOHNSY: He really is a dear, isn't he?

SUE: He seems to care a lot about us. Maybe someday he'll let us see his paintings.

JOHNSY: Oh, I hope so.

SUE: Too bad he isn't a successful artist.

JOHNSY: How do you know that?

SUE: Would he be living in this building if he were? *(They laugh.)* You know, I think that fuzzy old bear put gin in our coffee! I'm feeling a little giddy.

JOHNSY: I don't think it will hurt us! The light is so nice today. I'm going to get started on a new canvas.

(She puts canvas on easel.)

SUE: What are you going to paint?

JOHNSY: Well, I want to save my new tube of blue – let me see – that vine out there. Green paint is cheap!

SUE: *(Taking out a fashionable but humorous spring hat of the period with lots of feathers on it.)* Do you mind wearing this hat while you paint and letting me sketch? I'm getting good money from Wanamaker's for the sketches. I'll pay you a modeling fee.

JOHNSY: *(Taking hat.)* No! No! I only charge for strangers. You're my friend.

SUE: Are you sure?

JOHNSY: *(Putting hat on and posing.)* A regular Mrs. Astor, no? *(They burst out laughing.)* You know, I think you're right! I'm feeling giddy, too! – Oh, well: Art is Life! Life is Art!

BOTH:

(Sing a capella, Music Cue #5a.)

TO ART! TO ART!

LET'S SING A SONG TO ART!

SUE:

WE WORK ALL DAY

JOHNSY:

FOR LITTLE PAY

BOTH:

BUT STILL WE SING TO ART! ART!

LET'S SING A SONG TO ART!

(They laugh and then settle into work with SUE sketching JOHNSY as she paints with the hat on. A few moments go by.)

SUE: You have such a pretty neck.

JOHNSY: *(Laughs and touches her neck.)* Do you really think so?

SUE: Like a swan's.

JOHNSY: *(Blowing feathers on hat.)* Well, some kind of bird, that's for sure!

SUE: You'll be my little bird.

(Some more moments pass.)

JOHNSY: Sue?

SUE: Hmmmmmmm?

JOHNSY: Do you believe in hell?

SUE: Good heavens! What a question! Why are you thinking about such things?

JOHNSY: I always think dark thoughts when I paint.

SUE: But this is a beautiful spring day – and you're painting that vine out there. It's green and alive.

JOHNSY: Yes ... but autumn will come soon enough, and then winter – and what will happen then? The vine will turn brown and dry up. The vine will die.

SUE: Who's to say it won't make it to spring? My goodness, you have a morbid streak!

JOHNSY: I wonder if young women like us will ever be successful in the "Art World."

SUE: We will if we keep trying.

JOHNSY: I suppose you're right ... But in the end, I don't really care.

SUE: What? Don't you want to be famous?

JOHNSY: Nope.

SUE: And praised by all the art critics for "brilliant originality?"

JOHNSY: Nope.

SUE: And have your paintings hung in all the great galleries?

JOHNSY: Nope. Nope.

SUE: And make thousands upon thousands of dollars?

JOHNSY: Nope. Nope. Nope. *(MUSIC CUE #6. Sings.)*

SOME PEOPLE WISH FOR MONEY
TO LIVE IN LUXURY
TO WINE AND DINE
UPON BONE CHINA
FROM ACROSS THE SEA

SOME PEOPLE YEARN FOR POWER
A MONARCH THEY WOULD BE
TO RULE THEIR REALM
AND OVERWHELM US
WITH THEIR PEDIGREE

BUT ME, I LIKE THINGS SIMPLE
NO SATIN EVENING GOWN
NO VELVET GLOVES
NO CHELSEA FLAT
NO PERSIAN RUG
NO PERSIAN CAT
I JUST WANT TO BE IN
A CERTAIN EUROPEAN TOWN:

I WANT TO PAINT THE BAY OF NAPLES
TRAVEL TO ITALY (ONE TIME AT LEAST)
AND GAZE UPON THE BAY OF NAPLES
WATCHING THE GOLDEN SUN COLOR THE EAST
THAT'S ALL I ASK
THEN I WOULD BE HAPPY

PERHAPS I'D TAKE A LOVER IN NAPLES
RENT A SMALL VILLA AND LIVE WITH HIM THERE
WE'D DINE AL FRESCO IN THE COOL GARDEN
LEAVES OF GREEN LAUREL I'D WEAVE IN HIS HAIR
THAT'S ALL I ASK
THEN I WOULD BE HAPPY

WHY DO MY DREAMS NEVER COME TRUE?
WHY DO I PAINT MY SKIES GRAY AND NOT BLUE?
WHY DO I FEAR MY YEARS WILL BE FEW?
WHY AM I TELLING THESE BAD THINGS TO YOU?!

I JUST WANT TO PAINT THE BAY OF NAPLES
STAND AT MY EASEL AND TAKE IN THE VIEW
AND SEE MT. VESUVIUS RISE ABOVE NAPLES
OVER THE MEDITERRANEAN BLUE
THAT'S ALL I ASK
THEN I WOULD BE HAPPY ...

END OF SCENE ONE

SCENE TWO

(As lights fade on JOHNSY and SUE, they come up more on DOCTOR. MUSIC CUE #7 on word "November".)

DOCTOR: That was April. In November a cold, unseen stranger, whom we doctors call Pneumonia, stalked about the colony, touching one here and there with his icy fingers. Over on the east side this ravager strode boldly, smiting his victims by scores, but his feet trod slowly through the maze of the narrow and moss-grown "places" of Greenwich Village. Mr. Pneumonia was not what you would call a chivalric old gentleman. A mite of a little woman whose only dream was to paint the Bay of Naples was hardly fair game for the red-fisted, short-breathed old duffer. But Johnsy he smote; and she lay, scarcely moving, on her painted iron bedstead, looking through the window-panes at the blank side of the next brick house.

(Lights come up on JOHNSY in bed, sick, and SUE wringing out a cloth at the sink for JOHNSY's forehead. The window curtains are open, the vine is now slightly withered and losing leaves now and then as the wind blows. It is definitely November in New York.)

SUE: *(Bringing cloth.)* Here, my little bird. This will cool you. I've called for the doctor.

DOCTOR: This is where I come in.

(He knocks on apartment door.)

SUE: *(Letting him in.)* Oh, Doctor Fletcher! I'm so glad to see you!

DOCTOR: How is she today?

SUE: Not very good, I'm afraid. She won't touch her broth, and she's as hot as a fire.

DOCTOR: *(Going to bedside.)* How's my patient today, hmmmm?

JOHNSY: I'm hot, Doctor Fletcher. And I'm so tired. *(He pats her hand and turns to speak to SUE.)* Doctor?

DOCTOR: What, my dear?

JOHNSY: Do you believe in hell?

DOCTOR: No, I don't. And that's not something you should be thinking about. Now go to sleep. *(He takes SUE into the hallway.)* It's best if we don't move her. She has one chance in – let's say ten. And that chance is for her to want to live. Your little lady has made up her mind that she's not going to get well. Does she have any hopes, any wishes? .

SUE: She – she wanted to paint the Bay of Naples some day.

DOCTOR: Paint? That's good! See if she wants to do a little work! Medicine can only do so much. But get her to paint – or to ask about the new winter style in cloak sleeves, well! Then I will promise you a one in five chance for her, instead of one in ten.

SUE: Yes, thank you, doctor ... I'm sorry to ask this, but, *(She pulls out a sketch from behind her back.)* We're so short on cash. Could you accept this sketch as payment for this visit? It's Johnsy when she was well.

DOCTOR: In a hat with a lot of feathers! ... Of course, my dear. I am honored to have it. I'll be back this afternoon. Now try and get some rest yourself.

SUE: Don't worry about me, doctor. Thank you so much!

(DOCTOR exits and returns to watching the play. SUE breaks down in the doorway and cries her eyes out into a Japanese napkin until it falls apart and she throws it down. She composes herself and returns to the room, la-dee-dahing recognizable parts of "Bay Of Naples" as she swaggers over to JOHNSY in bed. JOHNSY is motionless with her face to the window. SUE stops singing when she believes JOHNSY is asleep. SUE goes to her part of the room and sets up to sketch by placing another wild woman's hat, winter style this time, on the bust/head of her mother. She starts to sketch. A few leaves begin to flutter down from the vine outside the window as music starts. MUSIC CUE #8.)

JOHNSY: Thirteen ... twelve ... eleven ...

(SUE hears her, gets up and tries to figure out what's happening.)

SUE: What is it, my little bird?

JOHNSY: Ten ... They're falling faster now. Three days ago there were almost a hundred. It made my head ache to count them. But now it's easy ... There goes another one. There are only nine left now.

SUE: Nine what, dear? Tell your Sudie.

JOHNSY: Leaves. On the Ivy vine. When the last one falls I must go, too. I've known that for three days. Didn't the doctor tell you? *(Sings.)*
WHEN THE LAST LEAF FALLS
FROM THE VINE UPON THE WALLS
I'LL BE DEAD
WHEN THE LAST LEAF FALLS
FROM THE VINE UPON THE WALLS
I'LL BE DEAD

AND MY HEART IS FULL OF DARKNESS
FOR MY BODY ACHES WITH PAIN
AND I KNOW THAT I WILL NEVER LIVE
TO SEE THE SPRING AGAIN

(Another leaf flutters from the vine.)

EIGHT LEAVES! AH – – –
SEVEN LEAVES! AH – – –
AND TOMORROW
THERE'LL BE NO LEAVES LEFT AT ALL

(The music continues.)

SUE: Oh, I never heard of such nonsense! What have old ivy leaves got to do with your getting well? And you used to love that vine, so, you naughty girl. Don't be a goosey. Why the doctor told me that your chances of getting well real soon were – let's see exactly what he said – he said the chances were – nine out of ten! Why that's almost as good a chance as we have in New York when we ride on the street cars or walk past a new building. Try to take some broth now, and let Sudie go back to her drawing, so she can sell the editor man with it, and buy port wine for her sick child and pork chops for her greedy self.

JOHNSY: You needn't get any more wine ... There goes another ... No, I don't want any broth. That leaves just five. I want to see the last one fall before it gets dark. Then I'll go, too.

SUE: Johnsy, dear, will you promise me to keep your eyes closed, and not look out the window until I am done working? *(Sings.)*
JOHNSY, YOU'RE NOT LIKE THAT VINE:
YOU'RE ALIVE! YOU'RE ALIVE!
JOHNSY, YOU MUST FIND THE WILL
TO SURVIVE, TO SURVIVE

FOR THE SUN WILL SHINE TOMORROW
AND ITS WARMTH WILL EASE YOUR PAIN
AND I KNOW IT'S TRUE
THAT YOU WILL LIVE
TO SEE THE SPRING AGAIN

SUE: *(Speaks.)*
Dear, dear! Think of me, if you won't think of yourself. What would I do without you? Tell me, my little bird, what would I do?

JOHNSY: *(Sings.)*
FOUR LEAVES!
AH –
THREE LEAVES!
AH –

JOHNSY:
AND TOMORROW
THERE'LL BE NO LEAVES LEFT AT ALL

JOHNSY:
AND MY HEART IS FULL OF
  DARKNESS
FOR MY BODY ACHES WITH PAIN

AND I KNOW THAT I WILL NEVER
  LIVE

SUE:
TOMORROW

SUNSHINE WILL
  EASE
YOUR PAIN, YOU
  WILL LIVE

TO SEE THE SPRING AGAIN   TO SEE THE
                                       SPRING AGAIN
AH! – – –   AH! – – –

(During the cadenza, JOHNSY gets out of bed and makes it to the window where she collapses. SUE helps her back to bed.)

JOHNSY:
WHEN THE LAST LEAF FALLS
FROM THE VINE UPON THE WALLS
I'LL BE DEAD
WHEN THE LAST LEAF FALLS
FROM THE VINE UPON THE WALLS
I'LL BE DEAD
    BOTH:
AND TOMORROW
THERE'LL BE NO LEAVES LEFT AT ALL ...

    SUE: Come, my angel. Let's get you back to bed.

    JOHNSY: I want to see the last one fall. I'm tired of waiting. I'm tired of thinking. I want to turn loose my hold on everything, and go sailing down, down, just like one of those poor, tired leaves.

(SUE draws the drapes over the window.)

    SUE: There now. Isn't that better? ... You'll be fine by tomorrow, my darling, I just know it.

    JOHNSY: There is no tomorrow for me.

(MUSIC CUE #9.)

    SUE: Hush, now. Don't say such things. Of course there's tomorrow. We have so much to look forward to. *(Sings, while wiping JOHNSY's forehead with a wet cloth, or some other tending gesture.)*
TOMORROW WHEN YOU'RE FEELING WELL AGAIN
WE'LL RIDE THE SUBWAY UP TO CENTRAL PARK

WE'LL RENT A BOAT, WE'LL SKETCH THE POND AND
    THEN
WE WON'T COME HOME TILL SOMETIME AFTER DARK

WE'LL LIGHT THE STOVE AND MAKE OURSELVES A
    MEAL
WE'LL PULL THE DRAPES AND PUT SOME CANDLES
    'ROUND
WE'LL TALK AS FRIENDS ABOUT THE WAY WE FEEL
THEN NESTLE ARM IN ARM WITHOUT A SOUND

MY LITTLE BIRD, HAVE FAITH IN WHAT I SAY
I'M CERTAIN THAT YOU'LL SOON BE OUT OF PAIN
YOU'LL FLAP YOUR WINGS AND FIN'LLY FLY AWAY
TOMORROW WHEN YOU'RE FEELING WELL AGAIN
TOMORROW WHEN YOU'RE FEELING WELL AGAIN

END SCENE TWO

SCENE THREE

(Off stage we hear BEHRMAN who is quite drunk, singing "Ode To Joy" MUSIC CUE #10. This continues as underscore up until he enters.)

JOHNSY: I hear voices, Sudie. Are those the angels?
SUE: No, dear. Just old Mr. Behrman, drunk in the middle of the day.

(She begins to collect her sketch book and pencils. Plus a very comical German mountain hat with a huge feather in it.)

DOCTOR: No more being locked away for weeks at a time for Mr. Behrman! After that first meeting he visited Sue and Johnsy every day and came to regard himself as an especial mastiff-in-waiting to protect the two young artists.
SUE: I'm supposed to sketch him for an ad this afternoon.

DOCTOR: He earned a little money by occasionally serving as a model to those young artists who could not pay the price of a professional.

SUE: But I think I'll cancel today. It would bother you for us to do it here.

(BEHRMAN stops singing and raps on the door. SUE opens the door.)

BEHRMAN: Guten tag. Guten tag. Guten tag. I have come for der session. Do I look like der beer-drinker for your ad?

SUE: Ssshhh!! Mr. Behrman. Johnsy is very ill.

BEHRMAN: Vat!? Der lettle Yohnsy? Let me zee –

SUE: No, Mr. Behrman. The doctor insists. She must rest.

BEHRMAN: Ach, Vat do doctors know!?

SUE: No, Mr. Behrman.

BEHRMAN: But I bring her new tube of paint! *(Pulls it out of pocket.)* Cadmium Yellow. Like de sun on a bright summer day!

SUE: I'll give it to her.

BEHRMAN: Has she stopped painting?

SUE: What?

BEHRMAN: She promised me she would never stop painting.

SUE: Mr. Behrman, I think you'd better go home now. Let's cancel for today.

BEHRMAN: Nein! Nein! I have an idea! Vee vork in my place, Ja! I finally invite you to my place!

SUE: Well – I don't –

BEHRMAN: Ja! Ja! Let Yohnsy rest.

SUE: Well – alright ... I need that sketch – *(She gathers things and crosses to JOHNSY.)* I guess I could leave you alone for awhile, couldn't I? I won't be long, my white rabbit. You try and get some rest.

(She kisses JOHNSY on forehead and follows BEHRMAN into the hall. MUSIC CUE #11.)

BEHRMAN: *(Sings, with a German accent.)*
COME INTO MY HUMBLE ABODE

YOU'RE MOST WELCOME
MY 'CROSS-THE-HALL NEIGHBOR
AS YOUR PRESENCE YOU'VE KINDLY BESTOWED,
    BESTOWED
I'LL SHOW YOU THE FRUITS OF MY LABOR
MY LABOR, MY LABOR
I'LL SHOW YOU, I'LL SHOW YOU
THE FRUITS OF MY LABOR

(BEHRMAN ushers her into his studio, and during the next "chorale" section, he keeps showing her to different places to sit that will have the best vantage of his draped canvas which is on an easel.)

I'VE PAINTED A GREAT WORK OF ART
A MASTERPIECE IN ITS OWN RIGHT
I'M GLAD YOU CAN SHARE IN MY JOY
AT THIS GRAND OCCASION TONIGHT

SO LET THE UNVEILING BEGIN!
OH, MY DEAR LITTLE 'CROSS-THE-HALL NEIGHBOR
RELAX, TAKE A SEAT
HAVE SOME GIN, SOME GIN
I'LL SHOW YOU THE FRUITS OF MY LABOR
MY LABOR, MY LABOR
RELAX, TAKE A SEAT
HAVE SOME GIN, SOME GIN
I'LL SHOW YOU THE FRUITS OF MY LABOR

(On the last beat of the song, BEHRMAN whips off the drop cloth on the painting to reveal a blank canvas.)

SUE: But Mr. Behrman! It's a blank canvas!

BEHRMAN: I am fully aware of it.

SUE: Why are you showing me this? All this time I thought you were a great artist.

BEHRMAN: Ja, ja. I were a great artist. Den I just stopped! And I don't know why ... You and Yohnsy. You are de great artists.

Dat is vhy you must convince her to keep painting no matter vhat
... I am nothing. She must get vell and continue to go on, because
I can not.

SUE: Of course you can, Mr. Behrman. We all have to go on.

(Music begins. MUSIC CUE #12.)

BEHRMAN: Nein ... nein ... *(He sings.)*
I'M A FAILURE IN ART
A FAILURE IN ART
FOR FORTY-FIVE YEARS
I'VE ATTEMPTED TO START
I PICK UP MY PALLET, MY BRUSH AND MY KNIFE
BUT I CAN'T PAINT A PAINTING TO SAVE MY LIFE (hic)
AND I DON'T KNOW WHY (hic)
AND I DON'T KNOW WHY
I'M A FAILURE, A FAILURE
A FAILURE IN ART (hic)

EARLY EACH MORNING I SQUEEZE OUT SOME RED
AND I MIX IT WITH BLUE
MAKING A PURPLE AS PERFECT
AS ANY DUTCH MASTER COULD DO
UP TO MY CANVAS I SAUNTER
WITH PALLET AND BRUSHES IN TOW
ONLY TO FREEZE IN MY FOOT STEPS
FOR REASONS I NEVER WILL KNOW
GOTT IN HIMMEL, GOTT IN HIMMEL
GOTT IN HIMMEL, GOTT IN HIMMEL (Belch)
SUE:
(Touching him.)
BUT SOMEDAY WHEN YOU'RE READY
YOU'LL PAINT YOUR MASTERPIECE
WITH BRUSH STROKES STRONG AND STEADY
YOUR GENIUS YOU'LL RELEASE
LIKE ALL THE WELL KNOWN MASTERS
YOUR PRAISES WILL BE SUNG
AND THEN THE NAME OF BEHRMAN WILL BE HEARD

ON EVERY MORTAL'S TONGUE
    BEHRMAN:
I'M A FAILURE IN LIFE
A FAILURE IN LIFE
I DON'T HAVE A JOB
AND I DON'T HAVE A WIFE
WITH NO INSPIRATION MY FUTURE IS DANK
I SEARCH FOR IDEAS BUT I COME UP BLANK (hic)
AND I DON'T KNOW WHY (hic)
AND I DON'T KNOW WHY
I'M A FAILURE, A FAILURE
A FAILURE IN LIFE (hic)

OFTEN AT NIGHT WHEN THE LIGHT
FROM THE LANTERN IS GOLDEN WITH GLOW
THERE TO MY EASEL WITH GREAT EXPECTATIONS
I EAGERLY GO
PLOTTING PERSPECTIVES AND ANGLES
I HALT WITH MY HEAD IN A SPIN
WANTING TO START
BUT NOT KNOWING JUST HOW I SHOULD REALLY
    BEGIN
GOTT IN HIMMEL, GOTT IN HIMMEL
GOTT IN HIMMEL, GOTT IN HIMMEL (Belch)
    SUE:
BUT SOMEDAY WHEN YOU'RE READY
YOU'LL PAINT YOUR MASTERPIECE
    BEHRMAN:
(Joins in, and takes over.)
WITH BRUSH STROKES STRONG AND STEADY
MY GENIUS I'LL RELEASE
LIKE ALL THE WELL KNOWN MASTERS
MY PRAISES WILL BE SUNG
AND THEN THE NAME OF BEHRMAN WILL BE HEARD
ON EVERY MORTAL'S TONGUE
ON EVERY MORTAL'S TONGUE
    SUE: I think we'd better cancel this session until you're feeling better. Besides, Johnsy probably –

BEHRMAN: Nein! Nein! Behrman is fine! I sit: you draw. I need der money. You need der money.

SUE: Very well, Mr. Behrman.

BEHRMAN: Art is Life! Life is Art! How do you vant me?

SUE: *(Setting up.)* Why don't you sit on that stool, like it was a rock by a stream. And could you wear this hat?

BEHRMAN: Ja, sure, my Zue. *(Puts on hat and poses.)* Like zees? *(SUE positions him after several funny poses. She begins to sketch and several moments go by.)* I vas vondering vhy I hadn't heard Yohnsy's laughter for awhile. Now I know. I miss der leetle angel.

SUE: She's very very ill.

BEHRMAN: You know, you should give her some of dis gin! *(Produces flask.)* Der medicinal qualities of der yuniper berry eez vell documented und I'm sure – *(She has begun to cry.)* Vat is it? Vat do you go crying like zis? You vill smudge der drawing.

SUE: The doctor says her chances are slim. She's very weak and the fever has left her mind morbid and full of strange fancies. *(SUE goes to window. Wind is blowing and snow is falling.)* See that vine out there? She's been watching the leaves fall off, counting them as they flutter down. When the last leaf falls she thinks she's going to die. What will I do, Behrman? What will I ever do? *(During this song, BEHRMAN listens and gets drunker on his flask of gin. SUE sings, MUSIC CUE #13.)*

LISTEN TO THE WIND
IT SINGS A SORRY SONG
IT KNOWS THAT SOON THE DARKNESS IS TO COME
FEEL THE BITTER WIND
IT'S COLDER BY THE HOUR
IT PENETRATES THE HEART AND MAKES IT NUMB
BUT I WILL NOT GIVE IN
I WILL NOT LOSE THE FIGHT
FOR JOHNSY'S WEAK
AND NEEDS ME THERE TONIGHT

I MET HER IN APRIL WHEN DAFFODILS BLOOM
WE POOLED OUR RESOURCES AND RENTED A ROOM

THROUGH WARM DAYS OF SUMMER OUR FRIENDSHIP
    DID GROW
AND THAT'S WHEN I LEARNED I LOVED JOHNSY, MY JO

I LOVE HER, MY JO

NOVEMBER CAME ON US WITH WINTER'S FIRST CHILL
POOR JOHNSY WAS FRAGILE AND SOON BECAME ILL
SHE'S COUNTING THE LEAVES ON THAT VINE AS THEY
    FALL
AND AFTER TONIGHT THERE'LL BE NO LEAVES AT ALL

I LOVE HER, MY JO
I LOVE HER
MY JOHNSY, MY JO

(The music continues.)

BEHRMAN: Dis eez foolishness. She chooses to die because de leafs dey drop off from a confounded vine? I have not heard of such a thing. *(He swigs some more gin.)* You must convince her to keep painting ... If she wants to give her life, let her give it to her work, not to some fool dunderhead like Mr. Pneumonia ... De leafs on der vine!? Vhy do you allow dat silly business to come in der brain of her? It's your fault –

SUE: I'm leaving now, Mr. Behrman

(She goes to leave, but he stops her.)

BEHRMAN: Nein! Nein! Come on! I sit: you draw! *(He sits again, and drinks again.)* Ach, you are just like a woman! I am ready to bose ... Gott! Dis is not any place in which one so great as Miss Yohnsy shall lie sick ... Someday I vill paint my masterpiece, and vee shall all go away. Gott in himmel ... yes ...

(BEHRMAN passes out at the end of this speech and slides to the floor. SUE looks at him and shakes her head. She gets an afghan and covers him on the floor. She gathers her things

*and goes back to her garrett and finishes the song to JOHNSY
who is asleep.)*

SUE: *(Sings)*
THE NIGHT WILL BE LONG AND THE DARKNESS IS DEEP
BUT HERE BY YOUR PILLOW A WATCH I WILL KEEP
MAY GOD AND HIS ANGELS LOOK DOWN FROM ABOVE
AND GUIDE YOU TO HEALTH WITH THEIR HEAVENLY
    LOVE

I LOVE YOU, MY JO
I LOVE YOU, MY JOHNSY
I LOVE YOU
MY JOHNSY, MY JO

(SUE pulls the curtains on the window.)

END SCENE THREE

SCENE FOUR

DOCTOR: I went back later and examined the poor girl ... *(He
enters the scene.)* But the prognosis was dismal. *(To SUE.)* Unless
there's a miracle she won't last until morning. See if she'll take
some of this. *(He hands SUE a bottle of medicine.)* And now, I
have to make some other calls.
    SUE: Doctor Fletcher?
    DOCTOR: Yes, my dear?

(She gingerly hands him another sketch as payment.)

    SUE: Can you take another sketch as payment?
    DOCTOR: Of course, of course ... It looks like you!
    SUE: *(Pointing to bust/head.)* My mother ... thank you.

(DOCTOR goes to leave then stops.)

DOCTOR: One last thing: It's so dreary in here! There's still some afternoon sun! Pull these drapes!

(DOCTOR quickly pulls drapes open and exits. The vine with its one last leaf is revealed, blowing in the wind. SUE is in a horror that JOHNSY will count the leaves again. She runs to the window, but is stopped by:)

JOHNSY: *(Not moving.)* Don't touch it, Sue.

SUE: But I –

JOHNSY: Please don't touch it. *(SUE stops.)* I want to see the vine. I must see the vine.

SUE: Johnsy, Doctor Fletcher was just here.

JOHNSY: What did he say?

SUE: He said that by tomorrow morning my Johnsy will be all well and laughing again. Now take this medicine he's left for you.

(JOHNSY refuses by turning her head.)

JOHNSY: Sudie, didn't the doctor tell you that I am that vine and that leaf? That during the night a gust of winter wind strong enough to break the tie will finally blow that leaf away? And off it will float ... off I will float, into the icy winter darkness ... forever unto oblivion ...

SUE: Go ahead and sleep. I'll be with you my darling. I won't leave you.

(SUE slowly pulls drapes shut on the window. MUSIC CUE #14.)

DOCTOR: How the wind howled that night! It blew through the little "places" of Greenwich Village like a banshee with a mission! The rain beat against the windows and pattered down from the low Dutch eaves. Woe to any leaf that had to cling to any vine! But Sue remained steadfast, watching over her sick friend like a guardian angel, putting cool cloths on her forehead and holding her hand. And then, the storm was finally over, the wind had died down, morning had broken.

JOHNSY: *(Sings.)*
SUDIE, OPEN UP THE DRAPES
I MUST SEE, I MUST SEE
    SUE: *(Sings.)*
I'LL GET THE CLOTH NOW
    JOHNSY:
SUDIE, OPEN UP THE DRAPES
AM I FREE? AM I FREE?
    SUE:
YOU'LL HAVE SOME BROTH NOW

JOHNSY:	SUE:
IF IT'S DEATH I MEET THIS MORNING	WE WILL
IT WILL COME AS NO SURPRISE	FIND JUST
SO PULL BACK THE BLIND	WHERE
AND LET ME FIND	YOUR
JUST WHERE MY FUTURE LIES	FUTURE LIES

(Music changes as SUE slowly pulls open the drapes. The leaf is still there! The music changes again and continues.)

SUE: Look! It's still there ... It's still there! The last leaf didn't fall. It's still there!

JOHNSY: How strange, Sudie. The last leaf didn't fall.

SUE: No, my angel, it hung on! The last leaf hung on! ... and if one little leaf can hang on, well, Johnsy, then so can you!

JOHNSY: *(After a few moments.)* You know ... I think I'll have that broth now ...

SUE: Yes, yes, my darling!

JOHNSY: And Sue? Hand me my comb ... I want to fix my hair.

SUE: That's my Johnsy! Oh ... what a happy morning!

DOCTOR: And that it was! I called on my friends as soon as I could. *(Stepping into the action.)* Well, my little lady, I think the worst is over. With good nursing you'll win! How do you feel?

JOHNSY: *(Sings.)*
I WANT TO PAINT THE BAY OF NAPLES
THAT'S ALL I ASK
THEN I WOULD BE HAPPY

(DOCTOR and SUE laugh.)

DOCTOR: That's my good girl! Now, I must go ...

SUE: Doctor Fletcher? *(SUE grabs a change purse from a table.)* Please take some money this time. *(She hands him a few coins.)* It's not much, but it's all we have.

DOCTOR: No, no. I couldn't. But I'll tell you what: I wouldn't mind another of your sketches. I think you're going to be famous someday.

SUE: Well ... How about this one? *(SUE hands him BEHRMAN sketch.)* It's old Mr. Behrman ...

DOCTOR: Dressed up like a beer-drinker ... *(DOCTOR moves SUE over to door, out of JOHNSY's ear shot.)* I have some sad news: Mr. Behrman died of pneumonia early this morning.

SUE: What?

DOCTOR: They found him *(He points out window)* right down there in the alley. His shoes and clothing were wet through and icy cold. And they found a lantern, still lighted, and a ladder, and some scattered brushes, and a palette with green and yellow colors mixed on it. Heaven only knows why he was out on a night like last night. Now I must go. You take care of Johnsy now.

(DOCTOR leaves.)

SUE: Of course, doctor ...

(SUE stares at the last leaf and moves slowly to the window. Music begins. MUSIC CUE #15.)

DOCTOR: *(To audience.)* And there you just about have it. It's amazing how faith, prayer and strong chicken broth can turn the tide in the worst sickness. What's even more amazing is how, every now and again, one life is so generous that it allows itself to be given up in place of another.

JOHNSY: Sue?

(SUE is still moving to window transfixed by the leaf.)

SUE: Yes, my little bird?

JOHNSY: What was the doctor saying over by the door?

SUE: *(Still transfixed, and she remains so to end of show.)* He said that old Mr. Behrman died early this morning.

JOHNSY: *(Who is now sitting up in bed knitting something.)* Poor Mr. Behrman. He was always so nice to us ... It's too bad he wasn't a successful artist.

SUE: Oh, but he was, Johnsy. *(She opens the window and feels the painted leaf with her hand on the brick wall, so audience knows it's painted.)* He was very successful ... He painted a masterpiece before he died. Old Mr. Behrman was a great artist. Perhaps the greatest of them all ...

(Pinpoint on leaf, the music swells ...)

THE END

FIN

KA-PUT

THE LAST LEAF—GROUND PLAN

CYCLORAMA

GROUND ROW

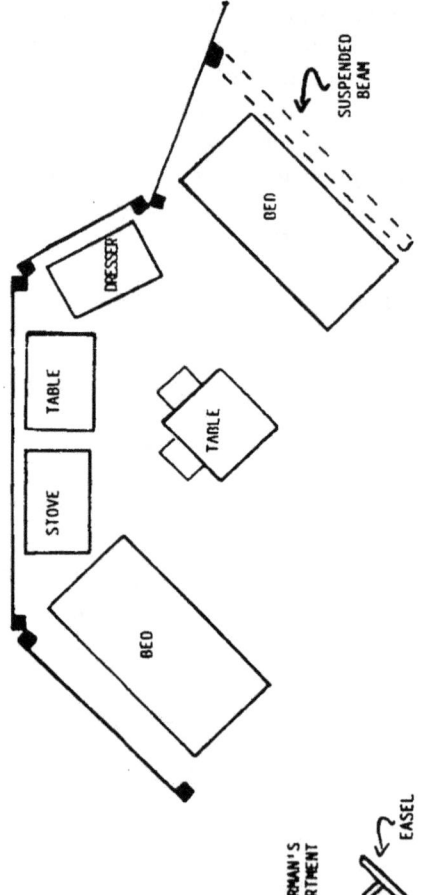

SUSPENDED BEAM

BED

DRESSER

TABLE

STOVE

TABLE

BED

EASEL

BEHRMAN'S
APARTMENT

EASEL

Actors Theatre of Louisville
The State Theatre of Kentucky

Jon Jory, *Producing-Director*

Presents

December 1 through the 26, 1981

O. HENRY'S

The Gift of the Magi

adaptation, music, and lyrics by

Peter Ekstrom

Directed by Larry Deckel

Musical Direction	Peter Ekstrom
Set Design	Paul Owen
Costume Design	Jess Goldstein
Lighting Design	Karl Haas
Co-Property Masters	Sam Garst
	Sandra Strawn
Stage Managers	Benita Hofstetter
	Craig Weindling

Cast of Characters

Della . . . . BEVERLY LAMBERT
Jim . . . . PETER BOYNTON

It is the Christmas Eve of 1905 in New York City.

This work is dedicated to Elizabeth Kelly.

CHARACTERS

DELLA — a young woman
JIM — her husband

TIME — 1905, the morning of Christmas Eve and that night

PLACE — Their one-room flat in New York City. They are very poor; the furniture is shabby. There is a bed with a chest at its foot, a dresser, a dressing table with a mirror (but for a theatrical effect there is no glass in the mirror), a kitchen table with two chairs, a small stove and sink, a small rocker and an armoire. There are two windows. Perhaps one looks out on to a brick wall, the other to the street if you were to look down. It is snowing.

NOTE: Care should be taken that this show be directed and acted as simply and honestly as possible.

The Gift of the Magi

MUSIC CUE #1 – "Mini Overture' segue to MUSIC CUE #2 –
"Opening Song" Lights come up. It is the morning of
Christmas Eve. DELLA, in camisole and bloomers, is at her
dressing table pinning up the last of her hair. JIM is in bed
under the blankets and sings his part in the following song
completely covered by them. There is some movement on his
part, but his face and body don't emerge until the end.

DELLA. (*singing*)
JIM, JIM, JIM DARLING
WAKE UP AND FACE THE DAY
(*There is no response from JIM. DELLA crosses to bed.*)
JIM, JIM, JIM DARLING
  JIM. (*singing*)
LEAVE ME ALONE! GO AWAY! GO AWAY!
  DELLA.
FACE THE DAY!
  JIM.
GO AWAY!
  DELLA.
FACE THE DAY!
  JIM.
GO AWAY!

(*During this next lyric, DELLA crosses to dressing table, gets*
empty pitcher and goes to the sink.)

DELLA.
JIM, IT'S TIME TO GET UP.
  JIM. (*almost a yawn but still singing*)
AH, AH, AH . . .
  DELLA.
TIME TO OPEN YOUR EYES.
  JIM.
AH, AH, AH
  DELLA.   JIM.
TIME TO LIFT YOURSELF   AH, IT'S COLD

45

UP OUT OF SLUMBER-   AND I WANT TO
    LAND.   SLEEP
JIM, IT'S TIME TO ARISE!   A LITTLE MORE.

(*DELLA pretends to fill pitcher with water in case JIM sees.*)

DELLA.
JIM, IT'S TIME TO GET UP.
    JIM.
AH, AH, AH . . .
    DELLA.
TIME TO GET OUT OF BED.
    JIM.
AH, AH, AH
    DELLA.   JIM.
IF YOU DON'T   AH, IT'S COLD
I WILL TAKE THIS   AND I WANT TO SLEEP
    COLD WATER
AND DUMP IT OVER   A LITTLE MORE.
    YOUR HEAD!
    JIM.
YOU WOULDN'T DARE.
    DELLA. (*She tiptoes to bed in time with music.*)
YES I WOULD!
    JIM. (*pokes his head out and sees the pitcher*)
YOU WOULDN'T DARE.
    DELLA.
YES I WOULD!

(*On this last "WOULD", DELLA lunges toward JIM. He leaps
    out of bed just in time. He is wearing faded and patched red
    long-johns as he says:*)

JIM. Wait! Della, stop!
DELLA. (*showing him the pitcher is empty*) Only fooling!
JIM. Ahh! I'll get you later!
DELLA. If you can!

(*MUSIC CUE: #3—"Tomorrow is Christmas". During this*

song DELLA is quite happy. JIM is a little sad, but not so sad that he doesn't smile now and then. This song is not a dance, but each should feel the music with their actions as they go about their morning rituals. Suggested activities: JIM stretches. JIM pulls his pants out from under the mattress. DELLA fills pitcher with warm water and pours it into JIM's washing bowl. JIM opens shutters. DELLA puts petticoat over bloomers. DELLA gets JIM's shirt from the back of a chair. She helps JIM with shirt, fastens cufflinks, etc.)

BOTH. (*They give each other a quick morning kiss on the first note of the song.*)
TOMORROW IS CHRISTMAS, THE TIME TO BE MERRY
WITH WREATHES TIED WITH RIBBONS AS RED AS A
  BERRY
THE CANDLES AND HOLLY CHASE WORRIES AWAY
FOR TOMORROW IS CHRISTMAS DAY . . .

TOMORROW IS CHRISTMAS WHEN SPIRITS ARE
  LIGHTER
THE SPARKLE OF SNOW MAKES THE CITY SEEM
  BRIGHTER
AND EVERYTHING LOOKS LIKE A WINDOW DISPLAY
FOR TOMORROW IS CHRISTMAS DAY . . .

LOOK OUTSIDE AND A STAR ABOVE
WILL SHINE AS A GUIDE TO US ALL
JOY WILL COME WHEN WE GIVE OUR LOVE
NO MATTER HOW GREAT OR HOW SMALL

A SMILE IN THE MORNING, A CHILD IN A MANGER
A GIFT FROM THE HEART TO A FRIEND OR A
  STRANGER
THE WARMTH OF A WORLD GETTING READY TO SAY
THAT TOMORROW IS CHRISTMAS, CHRISTMAS
  DAY . . .
TOMORROW IS CHRISTMAS DAY. . . .

(*At the end of the song JIM sits. DELLA goes to stove.*)

DELLA. Would you like a muffin, Jim? (*JIM rises and moves to dressing table.*)

JIM. I'm not hungry this morning, Dell, (*JIM sits at dressing table. There is a pause. DELLA is curious about JIM's response to her question. She hums or la-dee-dah's the tune to ".Tomorrow is Christmas" as she pours two cups of coffee.*)

DELLA. Some coffee? (*There is no response from JIM. Instead he is lathering soap and preparing to shave.*) Jim?

JIM. What?

DELLA. Coffee?

JIM. (*starting to shave*) Oh . . . yes, of course . . . coffee.

(*DELLA continues her humming as she crosses to the window, opens it, shivers and brings bottle of milk in from ledge. DELLA crosses back and pours milk into coffee.*)

DELLA. (*bringing coffee to him*) Darling, what is it? Didn't you sleep well? (*no response*) Jim!?

JIM. (*shaving throughout*) I love you, Dell.

DELLA. Of course you do! I love you too.

JIM. But what kind of a husband am I?

DELLA. (*crossing to bed to get her shoes*) Why, you're the best husband in the world!

(*During the next speech DELLA sits on bed and fastens one of her shoes.*)

JIM. Oh Della! Would the best husband in the world have his wife live in a fifth floor walk-up with only cold water complete with stained and torn furniture? Would he leave her there alone all day while he works at his job as a clerk in "NEW YORK CITY" that brought a meager twenty dollars a week which could barely pay the rent and the bills, let alone leave enough to buy food to keep her alive?

DELLA. Jim—

JIM. (*He turns and looks at her.*) Would the best husband in the world wake up to such a beautiful face on the morning of Christmas Eve knowing that he couldn't save, borrow or beg enough money to buy his wife a Christmas present? (*JIM nicks his lip. He is done shaving and begins to wash his face.*)

DELLA. (*crossing to him, one shoe on*) So that's it! . . . Jim, listen to me. When I married you and took your name, Mrs. James Dillingham Young (!) I knew things were going to be difficult for a while. But I loved you. And I love you now . . . and

tomorrow I'll feel just the same. (*She wipes excess soap off JIM's face.*) If it will make you feel any better, I can tell you that I don't have a Christmas present for you either! Now have a muffin, boy! See, we're not starving! . . . Come on, smile! (*DELLA sings to cheer him up.*)
'TIS THE SEASON TO BE JOLLY
FA LA LA LA LA . . LA LA LA
LAAAAAAAAAAAAAAAAAAEEEEEEEEEEEEEEEEH!

(*The last "LA" is rather a shriek, for when she hits it. JIM has jumped up and began to tickle her wildly. DELLA is the sort so ticklish that just to look at her tickle spots makes her burst into uncontrollable laughter. MUSIC CUE #4 — "Now I've Got You!" comes on this last "LA." Movement in this song should be fun, but not so wild that it interferes with very difficult singing. If this song proves too difficult for the players, a short tickle/chase scene may be substituted using lyrics from the song as spoken dialogue while JIM chases DELLA around their apartment.*)

JIM. (*sings*)
NOW I'VE GOT YOU!
    DELLA.
STOP IT! YAH HA HA HA HA HA
    JIM.
NOW I'VE GOT YOU!
    DELLA.
STOP IT! YAH HA HA HA HA HA
    JIM.
NOW I'VE GOT YOU!
    DELLA.
STOP IT YAH HA HA HA HA HA
    BOTH.
HA HA HA HA HA HA HA HA HA HA HA
    JIM.
WHAT'S THE MATTER?
    DELLA.
STOP IT! YAH HA HA HA HA HA
    JIM.
WHAT'S THE MATTER?
    DELLA.
STOP IT! YAH HA HA HA HA HA

JIM.
WHAT'S THE MATTER?
DELLA.
STOP IT! YAH HA HA HA HA
   BOTH.
HA HA HA HA HA HA HA!

JIM.	DELLA.
ALL I WANT TO DO MY DEAR	JIM! AH! NO! AH!
IS TOUCH YOU THERE AND TOUCH YOU HERE!	PLEASE, AH! STOP IT!
DON'T BE TIMID, DON'T BE FRIGHTENED	JIM JIM, NO NO!
DON'T YOU WANT TO HUG ME, DARLING?	PLEASE STOP! AAAHH!

   JIM.
NOW I'VE GOT YOU!
   DELLA.
STOP IT! YAH HA HA HA HA HA
   JIM.
NOW I'VE GOT YOU!
   DELLA.
STOP IT! YAH HA HA HA HA HA
   JIM.
NOW I'VE GOT YOU!
   DELLA.
STOP IT! YAH HA HA HA HA HA
   BOTH.
HA HA HA HA HA HA HA HA HA HA HA
HA HA HA HA HA HA HA HA HA HA HA . : . ETC.

(*They end up on the bed, laughing in a loving embrace.*)

JIM. Oh ... my Della ... you are so beautiful!
DELLA. (*blushing*) Jim!
JIM. Why are you blushing?
DELLA. Why do you think?
JIM. Tomorrow is Christmas ... will you wear your hair down
for me? (*There is a pause. JIM tickles DELLA again.*)
   DELLA. Anything!

(*During the next speech DELLA puts her other shoe on.*)

JIM. I love it when you wear your hair down. You have the

most beautiful hair in the world! (*with light-hearted pomp*) Why if the Queen of Sheeba lived in the flat across the airshaft, you would have to let your hair hang out the window someday to dry, just to depreciate Her Majesty's jewels and gifts!

DELLA. (*laughing*) Oh Jim! (*DELLA goes to chest to get her blouse. JIM to armoire to get his vest.*)

JIM. Della . . . I want so much for you . . . you know that?

DELLA. It will come with time, Jim.

JIM. Will it?

(*MUSIC CUE #4a — "Intro to If We Had Money".*)

JIM. (*continued*) I'm just so tired of being poor.

DELLA. It will come with time.

JIM. Yes, but — If we had money . . .

(*MUSIC CUE #5 — "If We Had Money". During the first lyrics of this song, DELLA puts her skirt on, and JIM helps her fasten it.*)

JIM. (*sings*)
IF WE HAD MONEY I'D BUY YOU A GOWN
MADE ALL OF VELVET AND LACE!
WE'D HIRE A CARRIAGE AND TROT THROUGH THE TOWN
AT A LEISURELY PACE . . .

DELLA.
WE'D STOP AT A RESTAURANT AND ORDER A MEAL
ASPARAGUS TIPS AND A BLANQUETTE OF VEAL
AND WE'D TOAST TO THE WONDERFUL WAY
    THAT WE'D FEEL . . .

JIM.
IF WE HAD MONEY.

BOTH.
IF WE HAD MONEY.

(*JIM gets his shoes and sits to put them on.*)

DELLA.
IF WE HAD MONEY I'D BUY YOU SOME SHOES
OF LEATHER IMPORTED FROM SPAIN!
WE'D TRIP DOWN THE AVENUE TAPPING OUR HEELS
TO A JOYOUS REFRAIN . . .

JIM.
WE'D STOP IN A BALLROOM WITH LIGHTS ALL
  A-GLOW
AND REQUEST THAT THEY PLAY EVERY WALTZ
  THAT THEY KNOW
AND WE'D SMILE ALL THE WHILE AS WE DANCED
  TO-AND-FRO
DELLA.
IF WE HAD MONEY.
  BOTH.
IF WE HAD MONEY.
  DELLA.
ALL I REALLY NEED, JIM
IS YOU CLOSE BY MY SIDE
  JIM.
IF WE HAD MONEY I'D RENT YOU A FLAT
THAT HAD CUSHIONS OF SILK IN THE CHAIRS WHERE
  WE SAT
AND BRIGHT REGAL BANNERS WOULD ALL BE
  UNFURLED
FOR IF WE HAD MONEY I'D BUY YOU THE WORLD!

DELLA.	JIM.
IF WE HAD MONEY	IF WE HAD MONEY
WE'D WORRY AND FRET	ALL CARES WOULD RETREAT
TRYING TO KEEP THIEVES AWAY	FOREVER SECURE WE WOULD STAY
INSTEAD OF THE BURDEN	INSTEAD OF THE BURDEN
OF BEING IN DEBT	OF MAKING ENDS MEET
WE'D HAVE TAXES TO PAY!	WE COULD GIVE HALF OUR RICHES AWAY!

JIM. (*picking up a stack of bills*)	DELLA.
THE COOKING AND WASH	
WOULD BE DONE BY A MAID	JIM, I DON'T MIND.
WE'D AWAKE EVERY MORNING	
AND BE UNDISMAYED	I'M HAPPY NOW!

FOR AT LAST ALL OUR
  BILLS
WOULD BE FINALLY
  PAID!
(*He throws bills in the air.*)
  DELLA.
IF WE HAD MONEY.
  BOTH.
IF WE HAD MONEY.

JIM.	DELLA.
ALL THE THINGS I WANT, DELL	ALL I REALLY NEED, JIM
TO KEEP YOU SATISFIED!	IS YOU CLOSE BY MY SIDE . . .

  DELLA.
IT DOESN'T MATTER, I'D STILL BE IN BLISS
IF YOU GAVE ME THE WORLD OR JUST GAVE ME A
  KISS
AND BECAUSE WE ARE POOR THERE'S NO REASON
  FOR SHAME
FOR IF WE HAD MONEY . . .
  JIM.
IF WE HAD MONEY . . .
  DELLA.
IF WE HAD MONEY . . .
I'D LOVE YOU THE SAME!
  BOTH.
IF WE HAD MONEY I'D LOVE YOU
LOVE YOU THE SAME!
(*They end the song in an embrace.*)

DELLA. What time is it, Jim? You don't want to be late for work.

JIM. I wish I could spend all day right here with my girl. But I suppose it is time for me to go.

DELLA. (*moving to stove*) Well take out your watch, darling, and see.

(*JIM turns his back to her and to the audience so no one can see the watch as he looks at the time and puts the watch back in his pocket.*)

JIM. It's seven-fifteen.

DELLA. Oh, good! (*a pause*) Let me look at your watch, Jim.

JIM. (*putting bow tie and armbands on*) Why?

DELLA. Because it's so pretty. We may not have money, but that watch is certainly a treasure for you. I remember when your mother gave it to you, after your father passed on. Let's have a look at it. (*JIM does nothing.*) Why are you always so embarrassed to take it out? It really is a treasure.

JIM. You know why . . .

DELLA. Because your mother lost the chain and you carry the watch on a leather strap? Jim! (*She laughs.*) Don't be a silly-willy! Come on!

(*MUSIC CUE #5a—"Watch Music." JIM starts to take watch out, and DELLA helps him. He holds it up in the air by the leather strap. There is a change of light, and the watch seems to glow!*)

DELLA. (*continued*) Oooooo! It's really quite a beauty, Jim. (*with light-hearted pomp*) You know, if King Solomon were our janitor, with all his treasures piled up in the basement, you could pull out your watch every time you passed, just to see him pluck at his beard from envy! (*They both laugh.*)

(*MUSIC CUE #6—"Look at my Watch". The lights change. The room lights dim. The special stays on watch. Special up on JIM's face. This song is JIM's internal sentiment. While he is singing DELLA straightens up the apartment, makes the bed and doesn't notice JIM. Again, for DELLA this is not choreographed, but she should feel the music and tone in her movements. JIM remains stationary throughout.*)

JIM. (*sings*)
LOOK AT MY WATCH
SEE HOW IT SHINES
IT ONCE BELONGED TO MY FATHER
IT'S MADE OF GOLD, WITH A FINE CHINA FACE
AND THE CRYSTAL HAS NO SCRATCH UPON IT . . .

SEE HOW THE HANDS
MOVE PAST THE NUMBERS
MARKING THE MINUTES AND HOURS
WITH STEADY PULSE THEY COUNT THE TIME

IF I WIND IT UP ONCE IN THE MORNING . . .
(*He sings to DELLA but she does not yet notice him.*)
MY LOVE FOR YOU SHINES JUST AS BRIGHT
IT'S PURE AS ANY GOLD COULD BE
WITH STEADY PULSE MY HEART COUNTS TIME
I DON'T HAVE TO WIND IT
IT NEVER RUNS DOWN . . .

(*DELLA sits at dressing table and applies finishing touches
   with powder puff in mirror.*)

I TOUCH YOUR SOFT HANDS
I LOOK AT YOUR FACE
I STARE IN YOUR EYES AND SEE
THAT YOU ARE MY ONLY REAL TREASURE
YOU ARE MY ONLY REAL TREASURE . . .

(*Now DELLA sees JIM's reflection in the mirror. She turns to
   him, and as she turns JIM looks back at his watch.*)

LOOK AT MY WATCH
SEE HOW IT SHINES
IT ONCE BELONGED TO MY FATHER
IT'S MADE OF GOLD, WITH A FINE CHINA FACE
(*Now JIM and DELLA face each other.*)
BUT YOU ARE MY ONLY REAL TREASURE . . .
(*Lights back to normal.*)

JIM. And now—(*He closes the watch with a snap.*) It really is
time for me to go to work. (*JIM goes to armoire to get his
jacket. DELLA goes to coat tree to get his overcoat.*)

DELLA. Don't forget your coat, Jim. It's cold out there. (*helping him into overcoat*) Maybe today they'll give you a promotion. Maybe today they'll make you President of the Company!

JIM. (*laughing*) I love you Dell.

(*JIM gives DELLA a quick goodbye kiss. MUSIC CUE #6a—
   "Money Underscoring". DELLA puts JIM's hat on for him.
   JIM exits.*)

DELLA. (*at door, calling to him*) Don't work too hard. Tomorrow is Christmas, and you won't have to work at all! (*DELLA
makes sure he's gone, then she runs to her secret hiding place*

and produces a can filled with pennies and proudly holds it up.)
Oh, Della! You are so sly. All this talk of being poor, when here
lies a fortune . . . (*She shakes the can, and the pennies rattle.*) in
pennies . . . but a fortune none the less! (*DELLA crosses to the
table and sits. She opens can and takes out a handkerchief and
places 'it flat on the table. She dumps out all the coins on this
handkerchief and begins counting them in tens over a musical
vamp.*) Ten . . . twenty . . . thirty . . . Jim is going to be so sur-
prised! . . . fifty . . . sixty . . . seventy . . . eighty . . . He doesn't
know it but . . . ninety . . . for five months I've scrimped at the
butchers, with the vegetable man . . . one dollar! . . . everywhere
. . . because this Christmas, more than anything . . . twenty . . .
thirty . . . I want to be able to buy Jim a gift — (*She pauses from
her counting and the vamp stops momentarily.*) a beautiful gift
. . . a gift worthy of the honor of being his. (*Vamp starts again.*)
sixty . . . seventy . . . eighty . . . one . . . two . . . three . . . four
. . . five . . . six . . . seven! (*She stands.*) One dollar and eighty-
seven cents! (*She suddenly realizes it's hardly anything and
makes a face.*) One dollar and eighty-seven cents. . . ? (*DELLA
sits down again.*)

(*MUSIC CUE #7 — "What Can I Give Him?"*)

DELLA. (*singing*)
I'VE SAVED THESE PENNIES FOR MONTHS UPON
    MONTHS
JUST TO FIND THAT THE SUM IS TOO SMALL . . .
I'VE TRIED MY HARDEST, BUT ONE-EIGHTY-SEVEN
WILL BUY NEXT TO NOTHING AT ALL
(*She rises.*)
DOWN IN THE STREET I SEE PEOPLE WITH PACKAGES
TIED UP IN SATIN BOWS
TREASURES THEY PURCHASED IN CHRISTMAS SHOP
    WINDOWS
AND NOW TAKEN HOME TO THOSE
THEY LOVE, TO THOSE THEY CHERISH
THEIR HUSBANDS, THEIR CHILDREN, THEIR
    FRIENDS . . .
(*She slowly walks around as she sings, stopping now and then.*)
BUT WHAT CAN I GIVE HIM?
WHAT CAN I OFFER?
WHAT CAN I GIVE HIM?
WHAT CAN THESE PENNIES BUY?

HOW CAN HE KNOW MY LOVE IS GOOD AS GOLD?
I WANT TO SHOW MY LOVE WITH SOMETHING HE
  CAN HAVE AND HE CAN HOLD

BUT WHAT CAN I GIVE HIM?
WHAT CAN I OFFER?
WHAT CAN I GIVE HIM?
WHAT CAN THESE PENNIES BUY?

WITHOUT A GIFT FOR HIM
MY HEART WILL SURELY DIE . . .

WHY ARE THESE PENNIES SO FEW?
(*She wraps them up in handkerchief.*)
THIS IS THE BEST I COULD DO . . .
(*She picks it up and carries it with her.*)
DOWN ON THE SIDEWALK I HEAR CHRISTMAS
  CAROLERS
SINGING A JOYOUS SONG
STANZAS THAT SPEAK OF THE SPIRIT OF GIVING
AND TELL US: IT WON'T BE LONG
BEFORE WE START THE HOLIDAY!
SOON WE WILL CELEBRATE!
CHRISTMAS IS HERE!

WHAT CAN I GIVE HIM?
WHAT CAN I OFFER?
WHAT CAN THESE PENNIES BUY?

AND I ONLY WANTED CHRISTMAS DAY
TO BE SUCH A HAPPY HOLIDAY
I DID MY BEST, I GAVE MY HARDEST TRY
BUT WITHOUT A GIFT FOR HIM
MY HEART WILL SURELY DIE
MY HEART WILL SURELY DIE . . .
(*DELLA ends the song at the bed. Sits with the music. And she is crying a little bit.*)

(*MUSIC CUE #7a—"What Can I Give Him—Underscore." DELLA rises and talks to herself.*)

DELLA. Well, Mrs. James Dillingham Young . . . you did what you could . . . Tomorrow is Christmas . . . and you have no present for Jim. You might as well not cry over something you can't do anything about. (*She sees herself in the mirror.*) Look how red and puffy your eyes are! If someone saw you right now they would think you had just found your little pet kitten frozen dead in the snow . . . (*This thought snaps her out of trance.*) My goodness! What a horrible thought! (*She puts bundle of pennies back in can.*) Tomorrow is Christmas . . . and tomorrow Jim will be home ALL day . . . and tomorrow I shall let my hair down . . . like this! (*She loosens her pins and her beautiful hair cascades to below her knees! There is a change of light, and her hair seems to glow! She picks up her brush and slowly combs.*) I really do love my hair . . . my mother once said it was too pretty to ever cut . . . and so I never have . . . I imagine someday it will grow so long that it could stretch all the way to . . . Brooklyn! (*She slowly rotates, playing with her hair.*) Jim loves it when my hair is down . . . He says I look as pretty and as graceful as a weeping willow . . . (*She smiles.*) I really do love my hair . . . (*Suddenly, an idea comes to her and flashes in her eyes.*) Wait a minute! (*Music stops.*) My HAIR!! (*Music starts again. Lights back to normal. DELLA runs about opening up drawers and furiously pulling things out in a mad search.*) Where did I put that card? . . . It must be here somewhere . . . Ah ha! Here it is!

(*She holds up an advertisement card and reads (sings) it off. MUSIC CUE #8 — "Madam Sofronie."*)

DELLA. (*singing*)
MADAM SOFRONIE, HAIR GOODS OF ALL KINDS
NEED A WIG? NEED A FALL?
DO NOT HESITATE TO CALL!
(*She speaks over music.*) Madam Sofronie's! It's on Fourteenth Street. I remember the hair-pieces in the window.
(*singing*)
IF YOU WANT THE MEN TO SMILE
WE HAVE JUST THE LATEST STYLE
GUARANTEED TO MAKE THE FELLOWS ROLL THEIR
    EYES
FOR A LITTLE BIT OF FUN
TRY A BRAID OR TRY A BUN
WE HAVE EVERYTHING IN EVERY SHAPE AND
    SIZE . . .
(*In small print at the bottom she sings:*)

BY THE WAY . . .
ALL OF OUR GOODS ARE MADE FROM GENUINE
  HUMAN HAIR
IF YOU NEED EXTRA CASH THEN STOP IN
AND MADAM SOFRONIE WILL PAY YOU
ACCORDING TO ITS BEAUTY
A VERY GOOD PRICE FOR YOUR HAIR.

(*MUSIC CUE #8a — "Melodrama".*)

DELLA. I knew I wasn't dreaming! There it is in print: "will pay
you a very good price for your hair" . . . a very good price . . .
Why, I'm sure I could get a small fortune for mine! And that,
plus my pennies would certainly be enough to buy a nice gift for
Jim! (*Music stops. She considers.*) I'll do it!!!

(*MUSIC CUE #8b — "End Scene 1." DELLA throws her hair
back, grabs the can of pennies, begins to put her shawl on,
hesitates for a second, then finally makes up her mind and
exits so that the door slams on the final beat of the music.*)

SCENE 2

*Segue to MUSIC CUE #9 — "Entre Scene". During this music
DELLA changes wigs offstage. Segue to MUSIC CUE
#10 — "Opening Scene 2". It is evening now, and the stage is
dimly lit. The stars have come out, and the fireplace glows.
DELLA enters with her shawl covering her hair. She is carrying a small wrapped package. She looks at it and smiles,
then crosses and places it on the mantle. She turns the switch
which lights the gas lamps, and the stage lights come up to
normal. She goes to dressing table and stands in front of the
mirror. She drops her shawl revealing her now short hair to
the audience. The music pauses.*

DELLA. Oh, my! (*Music again as DELLA grabs her brush and
furiously pulls it through her hair trying to repair the damage.
The music pauses.*) If Jim doesn't kill me before he takes a second look at me, he'll say I look like a Coney Island Chorus Girl.
(*Music again.*) But what could I do — oh, what could I do with a
dollar and eighty-seven cents? (*The music changes as DELLA*

says a little prayer.) Please God, please make him think I am still pretty. (*The slamming of a door is heard and JIM coming up the stairs la-dee-dahing the tune of "Tomorrow is Christmas." DELLA runs about as she says:*) He's home! Oh! Oh! Should I hide?

(*JIM's la-dee-dahing stops, and the music changes as DELLA makes one final touch in the mirror and positions herself for JIM's entrance. Music stops, door opens, and JIM enters carrying a wrapped present.*)

DELLA. (*aside*) Maybe he won't notice!
JIM. (*dumbfounded and dead-pan and standing still*) Dell. Your hair is gone.

(*MUSIC CUE #11 — "Your Hair is Gone!" During this song it is* absolutely essential *that JIM remains* totally dead-pan.)

JIM. (*singing*)
YOUR HAIR IS GONE
  DELLA.
PLEASE DON'T BE MAD!
  JIM.
YOUR HAIR IS GONE
  DELLA.
DOES IT LOOK BAD?

JIM.	DELLA.
YOURHAIRISGONEYOUR HAIRISGONE	LET ME EXPLAIN, JIM
YOURHAIRISGONEYOUR HAIRISGONE	LET ME EXPLAIN
YOURHAIRISGONEYOUR HAIRISGONE	LET ME EXPLAIN, JIM
YOURHAIRISGONEYOUR HAIRISGONE	LET ME EXPLAIN

(*JIM turns to leave, still holding his present, then turns around and enters again.*)

JIM.
YOUR HAIR IS GONE

DELLA.
YES EVERY TRESS!
    JIM.
YOUR HAIR IS GONE
    DELLA.
IS IT A MESS?

(*During this next lyric JIM places his wrapped present on the dressing table and crosses the room. DELLA follows. Then JIM turns around and focuses on her hair as DELLA backs away.*)

JIM.
YOURHAIRISGONEYOUR
    HAIRISGONE
YOURHAIRISGONEYOUR
    HAIRISGONE
YOURHAIRISGONEYOUR
    HAIRISGONE
YOURHAIRISGONEYOUR
    HAIRISGONE

DELLA.
LET ME EXPLAIN, JIM

LET ME EXPLAIN

LET ME EXPLAIN, JIM

LET ME EXPLAIN

DELLA. (*aside*)
COULD IT BE HE'S LOST
    HIS MIND?
HE KEEPS REPEATING
    WHAT HE SAYS
IS HE TEASING? IS HE
    SCOLDING?
IS HE GOING TO KILL ME
    ON THE SPOT?

JIM. (*to himself*)
YOUR HAIR IS GONE

YOUR HAIR IS GONE

YOUR HAIR IS GONE

YOUR HAIR IS GONE

    JIM. (*crossing to DELLA*)
YOUR HAIR IS GONE
    DELLA.
WHAT'S PAST IS PAST!
    JIM.
YOUR HAIR IS GONE
    DELLA.
IT GROWS SO FAST!
(*JIM sits in rocker and rocks in time to music.*)
    JIM.
YOURHAIRISGONEYOUR
    DELLA.
YESMYHAIRISGONEMY

HAIRISGONE	HAIRISGONE
YOURHAIRISGONEYOUR	MYHAIRISGONEMYHAIR
HAIRISGONE	ISGONEISGONE
YOURHAIRISGONEYOUR	YESMYHAIRISGONEMY
HAIRISGONE	HAIRISGONE
YOURHAIRISGONEYOUR	MYHAIRISGONEMYHAIR
HAIRISGONE	ISGONE

(*During the musical interlude JIM continues rocking in time. DELLA takes JIM's hat off and places it on the table. JIM holds his rock backwards when the music hesitates as if he is finally going to say something different, but then rocks forward again on:*)

JIM.
YOUR HAIR IS GONE
 DELLA. (*slightly annoyed now*)
YOUR EYES ARE GOOD!
 JIM.
YOUR HAIR IS GONE
 DELLA.
I UNDERSTOOD!
(*JIM leaves rocker and walks upright on his knees towards DELLA who backs away.*)

JIM.	DELLA.
YOUR HAIR IS . . . GONE	I'M STILL THE SAME, JIM
YOUR HAIR IS GONE	I'M STILL THE SAME
YOUR HAIR IS . . . GONE	I'M STILL THE SAME, JIM
YOUR HAIR IS GONE	I'M STILL THE SAME

(*JIM stays walking upright on his knees for half of the next lyric, but then is standing and by the dressing table.*)

DELLA. (*aside*)	JIM. (*focused on her*)
WHEN I TELL HIM WHY I CUT IT	YOUR HAIR IS GONE
WILL HE LOVE ME LIKE BEFORE?	YOUR HAIR IS GONE
WILL HE WANT ME? WILL HE NEED ME?	YOUR HAIR IS GONE
WILL HE TAKE ME IN HIS ARMS AGAIN?	YOUR HAIR IS GONE

(*JIM takes hand mirror-frame only, no glass, from dressing table and holds it up to DELLA's face.*)

JIM.
YOUR HAIR IS GONE
  DELLA.
PLEASE DON'T BE MAD!
  JIM.
YOUR HAIR IS GONE
  DELLA.
DOES IT LOOK BAD?

JIM.	DELLA.
YOURHAIRISGONEYOUR HAIRISGONE	YESMYHAIRISGONEMY HAIRISGONE
YOURHAIRISGONEYOUR HAIRISGONE	MYHAIRISGONEMYHAIR ISGONEISGONE
YOURHAIRISGONEYOUR HAIRISGONE	YESMYHAIRISGONEMY HAIRISGONE
YOURHAIRISGONEYOUR HAIRISGONE	MYHAIRISGONEMYHAIR ISGONE
YOUR HAIR IS GONE!	MY HAIR IS GONE!
YOUR HAIR IS GONE!	MY HAIR IS GONE!

(*The song ends, and JIM is staring at DELLA like a setter at the scent of a quail. It is an expression that she cannot read, and it terrifies her. It is not anger, or surprise, or disapproval, or horror — just a stare.*)

DELLA. Jim, darling. Don't look at me that way! I had my hair cut off and sold it because I couldn't have lived through Christmas without giving you a present. It'll grow out again — you won't mind will you? (*Pause. Jim just stares.*) I just had to do it. My hair grows awfully fast. Say "Merry Christmas," Jim, and let's be happy. You don't know what a nice — what a beautiful, nice gift I've got for you.

JIM. (*still dead-pan*) You've cut off your hair.

DELLA. Cut it off and sold it. Don't you like me just as well? I'm still me without my hair, aren't I? (*JIM looks under his hat on the table. Maybe he even looks in the stove.*)

JIM. You say your hair is gone.

DELLA. You needn't look for it. It's sold, I tell you — sold and gone, too. It's Christmas Eve, boy. Be good to me, for it went for you. Maybe the hairs of my head were numbered, but nobody could ever count my love for you. (*JIM wakes out of his trance and enfolds DELLA.*)

JIM. Don't make any mistake, Dell, about me. I don't think there's anything that could make me like my girl any less. Not a haircut, or a shampoo, or a shave . . . But if you'll unwrap that package—(*He points to dressing table where present is.*) you may see why you took me by surprise for a while there. (*DELLA runs to the dressing table, sits and opens the package excitedly . . . and there are The Combs! She lifts them in the air.*)

DELLA. Oh, Jim!

(*MUSIC CUE #11a—"Gift-Opening Music."*)

JIM. They're made of tortoise shell. They're the combs you had admired so many times in that little shop on Broadway, remember?

DELLA. Oh, yes, I remember. I worshipped these combs! But they were so expensive that I never dreamed that someday I could own them! Oh, thank you! They'll look so beautiful in—(*She suddenly remembers her hair is gone.*)—my hair!! Oh, Jim . . . (*DELLA makes a quick feminine change to tears and wails. JIM comforts her. DELLA recovers, and hugging the combs she looks up at JIM with dim eyes and a smile to say:*) My hair grows so fast, Jim! (*JIM laughs. Then DELLA leaps up like a little singed cat.*) Oh! Oh! I almost forgot! (*DELLA gets package from mantle.*) Look what my hair bought for you. (*She hands package to him . . . he hesitates.*) Go on! Open it! (*JIM opens the package and holds up the gold watch chain and fob.*) Isn't it a dandy, Jim! It's a gold chain and fob for your watch! I hunted all over town to find it. You'll have to look at the time a hundred times a day now! Give me your watch . . . I want to see how it looks on it.

(*The music stops. Instead of obeying, JIM turns and walks away a little. He then turns to DELLA and says:*)

JIM. Dell . . . let's put our Christmas presents away and keep them for a while . . . They're too nice to use just right now.

(*MUSIC CUE #12—"By the Way". JIM starts putting the presents away.*)

JIM. (*singing*)
BY THE WAY
IN ORDER TO PURCHASE THESE COMBS FOR YOUR
  HAIR
I NEEDED SOME CASH
SO I STOPPED INTO A PAWN SHOP ON BROADWAY
AND GOT WITH LITTLE TROUBLE
A VERY GOOD PRICE . . . FOR MY WATCH . . .
    DELLA. (*spoken over music*) Your watch is gone?
    JIM. Dell . . . You are my only real treasure . . .

(*They slowly walk towards each other. MUSIC CUE #13 —
   "End Scene 2".*)

BOTH. (*singing*)
ALL I REALLY NEED DELL/JIM
IS YOU CLOSE BY MY SIDE

IT DOESN'T MATTER, I'D STILL BE IN BLISS
IF YOU GAVE ME THE WORLD OR JUST GAVE ME A
  KISS
AND AS LONG AS I'M NEAR YOU MY HEART SHALL
  PROCLAIM
FOREVER AND EVER
FOREVER AND EVER . . . I'LL LOVE YOU THE SAME!
(*They end in an embrace.*)

(*MUSIC CUE #14- "Bows and Tomorrow Is Christmas (reprise)." When they begin the reprise JIM and DELLA take out
  strings of popcorn and snowflakes made of newspaper and
  decorate the flat as they sing. If doing with "THE LAST
  LEAF", BEHRMAN and SUE can come on and join in. Near
  the end of the reprise they produce a sprig of mistletoe which
  they hang from one of the gas lamps, and they end
  underneath it with a kiss.*)

BOTH. (*singing*)
TOMORROW IS CHRISTMAS, THE TIME TO BE MERRY
WITH WREATHES TIED WITH RIBBONS AS RED AS A
  BERRY
THE CANDLES AND HOLLY CHASE WORRIES AWAY
FOR TOMORROW IS CHRISTMAS DAY ...

TOMORROW IS CHRISTMAS WHEN SPIRITS ARE
    LIGHTER
THE SPARKLE OF SNOW MAKES THE CITY SEEM
    BRIGHTER
AND EVERYTHING LOOKS LIKE A WINDOW DISPLAY
FOR TOMORROW IS CHRISTMAS DAY . . .

LOOK OUTSIDE AND A STAR ABOVE
WILL SHINE AS A GUIDE TO US ALL
JOY WILL COME WHEN WE GIVE OUR LOVE
NO MATTER HOW GREAT OR HOW SMALL

A SMILE IN THE MORNING, A CHILD IN A MANGER
A GIFT FROM THE HEART TO A FRIEND OR A
    STRANGER
THE WARMTH OF A WORLD GETTING READY TO SAY
THAT TOMORROW IS CHRISTMAS, CHRISTMAS DAY!!
(*spoken*) Merry Christmas!!!

(*MUSIC CUE #15 — "Exit Music."*)

THE END

COSTUMES

JIM (humble clerk look)
Red union suit: — faded and patched
Red and white striped shirt
  period white stiff collar
  cufflinks
Sepia toned suit (worn looking)
  Cutaway coat
  Suspenders
  Vest with watch pocket
Bow tie
Bowler hat
Socks — heavy dark wool
Tattered gloves
Overcoat
Muffler
Ankle high brown shoes with hooks
Wire framed glasses (optional)

DELLA
Long wig
Short wig
Bloomers
Camisole
Corset
Petticoat
Period hose (black or brown cotton)
Shirtwaist blouse with high collar (ecru)
Floor length wool skirt
Period boots (with hooks)
Shawl

PROPERTY LIST

Furniture/set pieces (all period and humble):
Windows (at least one practical) — frosted
Snow machines
Window shutters (practical)
Bed — Mission or iron frame
Worn carpet
Chest
Armoire
Rocking chair
Hearth seat
Dresser with mirror frame (*no* glass)
Fireplace
Low sink
Stove
Coal bucket
Andirons
Cupboard
Kitchen table — round
2 kitchen chairs
Dressing table with splashboard and mirror frame (*no* glass)
Chair at dressing table
Coat tree
Props (practical — all must be period and humble):
Water pitcher
Wash basin
Bed linens
Bed spread: patchwork
Coffee cups
Coffee pot with coffee
Spoons
Milk bottle with milk
Shaving brush
Shaving soap
Razor: straight
Powder puff and jar
Hair pins
Brush
Muffin tin
Muffins
Hand towel

Dish towel
Hand mirror (frame only — no glass)
Broom
Sugar bowl
Stack of unpaid bills
Jar or can for pennies
187 pennies
Handkerchief for pennies
Madame Sofronie advertisement card
Wooden crate (small)
Strings of popcorn and newspaper snowflakes
Sprig of mistletoe
Gold pocket watch with leather strap
Two wrapped packages for The Gifts
Combs for Della
Gold watch chain and fob for Jim

Props (set dressing):
Clothes and linens in chest and armoire
Lumps of coal in coal bucket
Cupboard items: dishes, pots, pans, utensils, glasses, jars, food
    basics (salt, pepper, flour, coffee, etc.)
Toiletries on dressing table (tooth powder, talc, pomade — not
    too much)
A *few* evergreen branches on mantle and dresser
Bible

THE GIFT OF THE MAGI

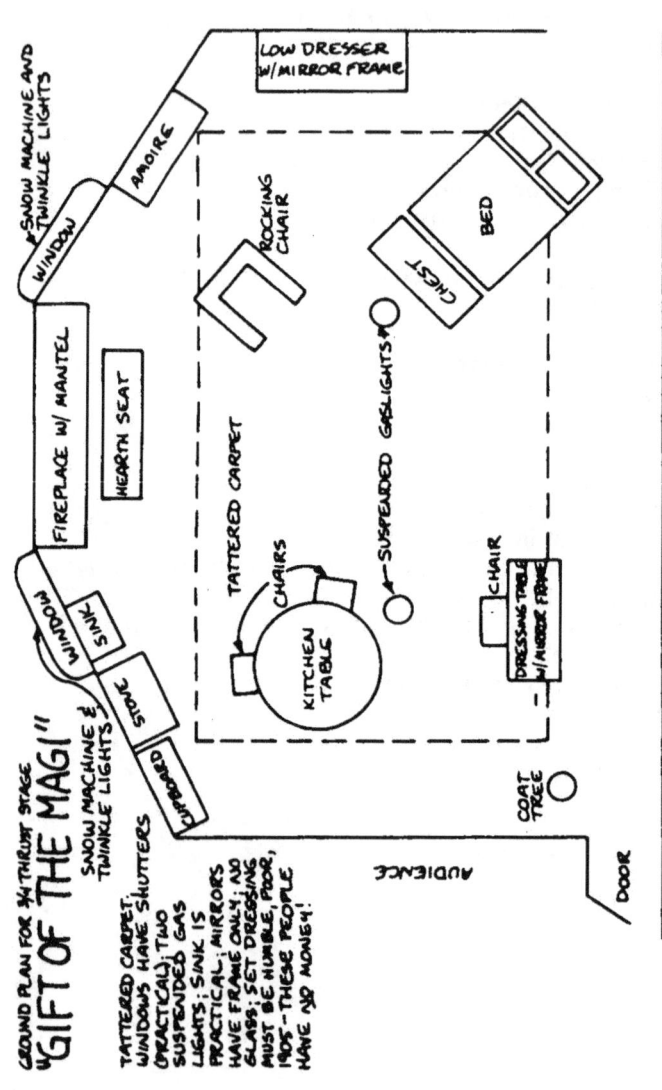

GROUND PLAN FOR 3/4 THRUST STAGE
"GIFT OF THE MAGI"

SNOW MACHINE & TWINKLE LIGHTS

TATTERED CARPET;
WINDOWS HAVE SHUTTERS
(PRACTICAL); TWO
SUSPENDED GAS
LIGHTS; SINK IS
PRACTICAL; MIRRORS
HAVE FRAME ONLY; NO
GLASS; SET DRESSING
MUST BE HUMBLE, POOR,
1905 — THESE PEOPLE
HAVE NO MONEY!

SNOW MACHINE AND TWINKLE LIGHTS

LOW DRESSER W/MIRROR FRAME

AMOIRE

WINDOW

FIREPLACE W/ MANTEL

HEARTH SEAT

WINDOW

SINK

STOVE

CUPBOARD

ROCKING CHAIR

BED

CHEST

SUSPENDED GASLIGHTS

TATTERED CARPET

CHAIRS

KITCHEN TABLE

CHAIR

DRESSING TABLE W/MIRROR FRAME

COAT TREE

AUDIENCE

AUDIENCE

DOOR

AUDIENCE

THE GIFT OF THE MAGI

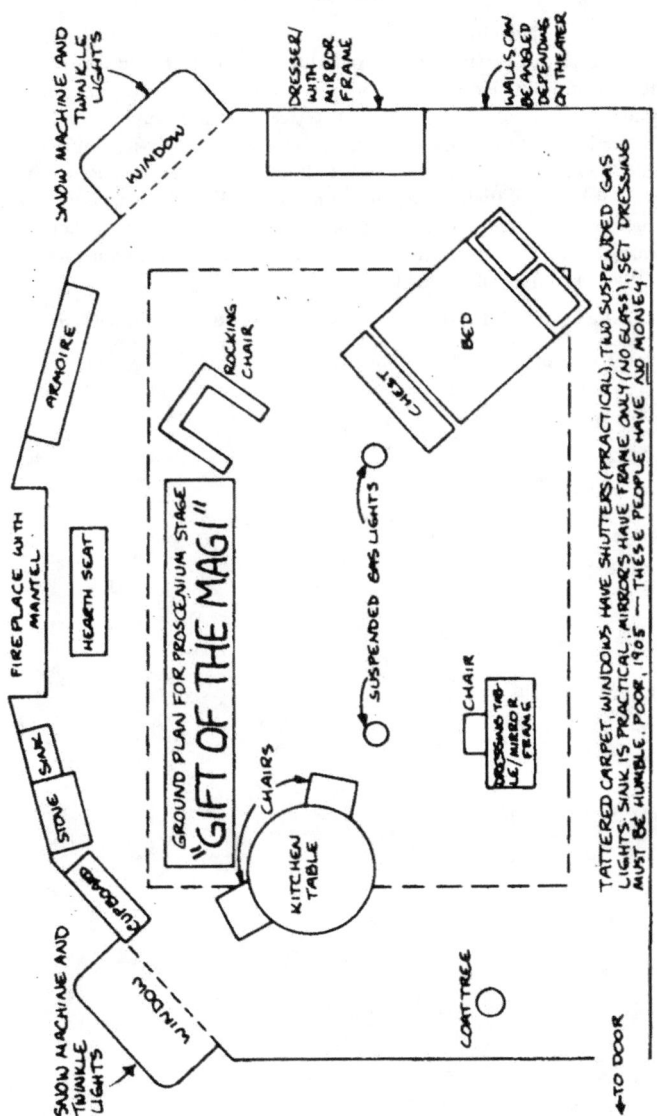

SNOW MACHINE AND TWINKLE LIGHTS

WINDOW

DRESSER/ WITH MIRROR FRAME

WALLS CAN BE ANGLED DEPENDING ON THEATER

ARMOIRE

FIREPLACE WITH MANTEL

HEARTH SEAT

ROCKING CHAIR

BED

CHEST

STOVE   SINK

CUPBOARD

GROUND PLAN FOR PROSCENIUM STAGE
"GIFT OF THE MAGI"

SUSPENDED GAS LIGHTS

CHAIRS

KITCHEN TABLE

CHAIR

DRESSING TABLE/MIRROR FRAME

SNOW MACHINE AND TWINKLE LIGHTS

WINDOW

COAT TREE

←TO DOOR

TATTERED CARPET, WINDOWS HAVE SHUTTERS (PRACTICAL), TWO SUSPENDED GAS LIGHTS. SINK IS PRACTICAL. MIRRORS HAVE FRAME ONLY (NO GLASS), SET DRESSINGS MUST BE HUMBLE. POOR. 1905 — THESE PEOPLE HAVE *NO MONEY!*

MUSIC USE NOTE

Licensees are solely responsible for obtaining formal written permission from copyright owners to use copyrighted music in the performance of this play and are strongly cautioned to do so. If no such permission is obtained by the licensee, then the licensee must use only original music that the licensee owns and controls. Licensees are solely responsible and liable for all music clearances and shall indemnify the copyright owners of the play(s) and their licensing agent, Samuel French, against any costs, expenses, losses and liabilities arising from the use of music by licensees. Please contact the appropriate music licensing authority in your territory for the rights to any incidental music.

IMPORTANT BILLING AND CREDIT REQUIREMENTS

If you have obtained performance rights to this title, please refer to your licensing agreement for important billing and credit requirements.

www.ingramcontent.com/pod-product-compliance
Lightning Source LLC
Chambersburg PA
CBHW070357120726
47909CB00008B/2890